A DATE FOR VALENTINE'S DAY

A MINNESOTA LAKES ROMANCE

ROSE MARIE MEUWISSEN

CONTENTS

A DATE FOR VALENTINE'S DAY

BY

Rose Marie Meuwissen

A Date for Valentine's Day

Print ISBN: 978-1-954-030-00-8
Published in the United States of America
Nordic Publishing
Edited by Leanore Elliot
Cover Design by Rose Marie Meuwissen

nordic
PUBLISHING

❀ Created with Vellum

To all those special Valentine's Day dinners for two with roses and chocolate whether they are spent at your favorite restaurant or at home.
May your Valentine's Day be filled with Love!

A MINNESOTA LAKES ROMANCE
NOVELETTE

Lake Minnetonka

A DATE FOR VALENTINE'S DAY

Maggie Johnson immensely disliked Valentine's Day.
Luckily, her mother was determined to change her mind.

The charity auction for a Valentine's Day
Dinner Date with one of Minneapolis' most eligible bachelors could
just be the solution.

But, would Maggie be open to finding someone to love on
Valentine's Day?

MINNESOTA LAKES

MINNESOTA

Land of 10,000 Lakes

A DATE FOR VALENTINE'S DAY

By

Rose Marie Meuwissen

*M*aggie Johnson's thoughts regarding the upcoming Valentine's Day holiday were mostly depressing, to say the least. Since her short lived marriage to Sam, who she thought was the love of her life, it was a holiday she'd just as soon skip. Especially, after catching him cheating with her best friend. At least, she'd thought Sue was her best friend, but most definitely, another mistake she'd made.

After all, it was a holiday geared toward couples and if you didn't have someone to be a couple with, it sucked! Last year, when the Bachman's delivery truck pulled up to make a flower delivery at her office on Valentine's Day, she wanted more than anything to hide in her office. Because, she knew she wouldn't get flowers. And sadly, she was just about the only one. It had unquestionably sucked to be her that day. She'd even thought about taking the day off this year to just sit home alone, order pizza and watch a sappy romantic comedy. By herself.

So when her mother, who always was trying to set her up with someone, called to politely request Maggie attend a charity event with her, she was unquestionably suspicious. It would be great fun, but not for her. Of all things, it was an auction for a 'Valentine's Dinner Date' with a local eligible business man. According to her mother, these men were "hot". Definitely husband material and she wasn't taking no for an answer. So, unfortunately, this meant Maggie would be going.

The event was being held at the Lafayette Country Club on Saturday night which was two weeks before Valentine's Day. All the money collected went to the Children's Hospital Heart Specialty Department. There was no denying it was a good cause. But, she had no intentions of going on a date with a man she didn't know, even if it was for charity. No, it just wasn't her style at all. But then again, the chances of her mother placing a winning bid were low if the upper crust of Minnetonka and Wayzata showed up to bid.

So if it pleased her mother to have Maggie accompany her to the event, she would do it. Her mother had offered to cover the purchase of, as she put it, 'something that would show off Maggie's great figure, and make her look sexy but still classy.' So here she was at the mall looking for the perfect, sexy, little black dress. Thankfully, her *new* best friend, Annie, came along to help.

"I think you should try these on," Annie said and handed five dresses to Maggie.

"Okay. And I found a couple, too." Maggie walked into the dressing room.

After trying them all on, she decided on one. A black short dress that looked like it was made out of spandex, she thought as she looked in the mirror. The dress clung to her body like a second skin. It had gold trim around the hem and the low V-neckline. She had to admit, she looked hot. So why didn't she have a boyfriend?

"Maggie?" Annie questioned through the door.

"Yes, I think this is the one," Maggie said as she walked out to show Annie, then turned and walked back into the dressing room to change back into her clothes.

"You don't look happy, are you okay?" Annie asked when Maggie came out carrying the dress.

"I don't know about this whole thing. My mother is most certainly going to bid on one of the dates and I get the feeling she will do just about anything to make sure she wins. Money isn't an issue to her when she wants something badly enough. And she will think it is money well spent, if she can make sure I have a date on Valentine's Day. Let's hope the wealthy of the Minneapolis area and its suburbs come out to support the cause and outbid her!"

"Sounds like fun to me. Do you think she would buy me a date, too?" Annie asked.

They both laughed.

"Probably not, but I can always ask," Maggie answered and walked up to the cashier's counter.

"Maggie, all you have to do is let her know which one looks good to you. That way you will be able to ensure you'll have a great date."

"But what if I don't like any of them?"

"That could be a problem, but if they are all eligible bachelors and local business men, there should be at least one out of twenty that you could spend a couple of hours with over dinner."

"I suppose. It just seems a little scary and mega stressful."

"You'll be fine. And just think of the possibility that maybe he'll be someone you could actually like."

"We can only hope. Don't assume this is even happening, though, because I'm praying it won't."

Maggie and Annie left the store and walked out to the car.

CHAPTER 2

*M*att Lindstrom stared out of his penthouse office in the Pentagon Office Park in Bloomington. The Nature Reserve Park across the street lay blanketed in white with a twelve inch snow pack covering the grass below. Light snow floated gently to the bare sidewalk below the window. What was to be expected? It was February, after all.

His last client for a financial planning appointment had just left his office.

Minutes later his dad walked into his office. "Ready for the big night?" Carl Lindstrom asked and took a seat in the chair facing Matt's desk.

"Dad, I can't believe I let you talk me into this. I know plenty of women who'd love to be my date for Valentine's Day."

"But this is for a good cause. Who knows maybe you'll meet someone who will be the 'One'? You never know."

"Awe Dad, you know I'm not looking to get married. At least, not right now."

"Can't an old man hope? I'm not getting any younger and

neither are you. I'd like to get some grandkids before I die," Carl stated.

"Dad, you're not that old and you certainly aren't dying any time soon. You're in perfect health."

"You never know. We could all be gone tomorrow."

"Let's hope not. Who would run the company?" Matt teased.

"See that's my point exactly. I need some grandchildren." Carl got up to leave.

"I'm leaving shortly to go home and change. I'll see you there," Matt said shutting down his computer.

"Just be open to this whole idea. Give the woman who wins a chance. Try to put her at ease. It's tougher for them."

"Yes, Dad. I'll be nice. You have my word."

As Matt strode out of the office building to his BMW, he couldn't help thinking this was one of the craziest things he'd ever done. Not even in college had he auctioned off himself for a date. No, in fact, he'd turned his fraternity brothers down when they'd asked him to do it for an Alpha Phi sorority auction. Recently, though, he'd been warming to the idea of finding that one special woman. Unfortunately, he hadn't met her yet. So, until he did, marriage and children were not in his immediate future.

So why was he doing this tonight?

For his dad, that's why.

$\mathcal{A}$fter applying the finishing touches on her makeup, Maggie slipped on the little black dress. She took a quick glance at her reflection in the full length mirror, liking what she saw. But would the men? Why did she even care? It was only one date. *For charity.* Heck, maybe her mother wouldn't have a winning bid and then all her fears would be for naught. What was she thinking? Her mother always got what she wanted and her mother badly wanted to get her a date for Valentine's Day.

She had no doubt in her mind that she would be going on a date with one of the eligible bachelors.

On her drive over to the Lafayette, she couldn't help feeling apprehensive. Thankfully, the snow stopped falling so there was only a light dusting on the road. She decided to use the valet service since she was dressed in a skin tight dress and heels. Plus, then they would brush the snow off the windshield for her before she went home. There were times when the valet service was definitely worth it.

"Mam, welcome to the Lafayette Country Club," the valet said and opened her door, offering her his hand as support to get out of the car. Then, handed her a valet ticket.

Maggie straightened her dress, pulling it down slightly as it had slid up while driving and pulled her long black wool coat together as a blast of icy winter wind hit her body full force. Walking quickly towards the front doors of the Lafayette Country Club, she opened her purse to slide the valet ticket inside. Unfortunately, with her head turned down she didn't see the man directly in front of her and she walked right smack into a solid manly chest. He smelled so masculine. "Excuse me. I'm so sorry. I wasn't looking where I was going," Maggie quickly apologized as she looked up into dark brown eyes framed by a chiseled face. His sandy blond hair had an impeccable cut suggesting his obvious wealthy background.

"Apology accepted," he replied gazing into her eyes.

Their eyes locked for what seemed to be only a moment, but felt like an eternity.

"I'd better be going. I'm meeting someone, and I don't want to be late." Maggie said in a rush eager to leave the unnerving situation.

He gallantly held the door open for her and she quickly walked away, praying her mother was already there. She admitted the need to be saved from an awkward moment she'd just experienced. But was it actually that or was it really that she'd truly felt something towards a man? She hadn't felt anything, since her divorce, for any of the men she'd met. Why, this man, who wasn't someone she'd really met? In fact, she had no idea who he was. Or, if she'd ever get the chance to be introduced properly to him.

She didn't dare turn around to see which way he'd gone without appearing blatantly obvious.

"Maggie," her mother called out and waved.

Thank heavens for her mother. Sometimes, she really

appreciated having her mother around and now was one of those times. "Mom, glad you spotted me. We never discussed where we were meeting," she said and hugged her mother lightly, as was their usual greeting.

"Who was that man you were talking to at the door?"

"I have no idea. I accidentally walked into him while putting the valet ticket in my purse. I think this whole date auction has made me extremely nervous about tonight. You know you don't have to buy me a date for Valentine's Day."

"I know but I want to, Maggie. It's something I can do for you. Maybe it will be a push towards getting you back out there dating. Who knows, maybe he could be the one for you? You never know. They're not all like Sam. Believe it or not, there are a lot of good guys out there, too."

"It's finding the good ones, that's the problem. Let's get this over with." Maggie motioned towards the door to the James J. Hill Ballroom.

"I just found out the people who signed up to be bidders are sitting in a reserved section in front of the stage. So here is your ticket for the observers section. Sorry, didn't know we wouldn't get to sit together."

"That's fine." Maggie took the ticket from her mother.

"Let's get a glass of wine and some hors d'oeuvres before the auction begins."

After filling their plates with bacon wrapped scallops, spicy steak medallions, grapes, raspberries and strawberries, they joined her mother's longtime friend, Nancy Carlson, who was the CEO of Nordic Traveler. Maggie grew up with Nancy's daughter, Liv, who had married well and moved to Seattle. She hadn't talked to Liv for quite a while, which was neglectful on her part, so she made a mental note to give her a call.

"Margit said you are willing to go on a date with one of

these bachelors?" Nancy questioned nodding toward her mother.

"It's for a good cause. What can a dinner hurt?" Maggie asked good-naturedly.

"Of course, it is. And it's only dinner. Most of these bachelors are quite accomplished young men and extremely good looking." Nancy smiled and winked at Maggie.

"Exactly. Just what I told her," Margit added.

"Might just find a keeper. I keep hoping you'll take a chance again. You deserve to be happy, Maggie," Nancy sincerely offered.

The conversation drifted towards Nancy's latest tour offerings and Maggie's eyes veered towards people watching the crowd of Minneapolis's elite. She had to honestly admit the room was filled with eligible bachelors. She knew some of them because they'd gone to high school together. Unfortunately, none of them had ever piqued her interest.

Maggie scanned the crowd for the man she'd bumped into. Finally, she spotted him conversing with a beautiful woman and laughing genially. She found herself staring at him and taking in every inch of his body. The feelings of attraction she felt toward him were intense.

She was sorely tempted to ask Nancy if she knew who he was, but that would show she was interested and she would never hear the end of it. Although, if Nancy knew him, she could get a formal introduction. No, that would be all she needed. Making the first move. It never went well for the woman to show interest first. Thankfully, she was saved by the bell, as the saying goes. The lights dimmed slightly and everyone moved to the Grand Ballroom to take their seats.

Maggie took her seat which happened to be next to Nancy. Her mother was ushered up to the front section where the bidders could have a closer view of the bachelors

participating in the auction. The room grew quiet in anticipation of the program about to commence.

First the MC introduced, Don Gunnersen, the president
of the Minneapolis Children's Hospital. With the formalities
over, they were on to the good stuff. The devastatingly handsome men. Maggie actually found herself looking forward to
hearing the profiles of each man. Twenty men equaled
twenty lucky women who would enjoy a dinner date on
Valentine's Day. At least she was sure most women would
consider it to be a highly prized date.

One by one the men took the stage while the MC read
their bio profiles and on the large screen behind them
pictures flashed of their companies and other charities they
supported. At the end, each bachelor took the mic to say a
few words about why they'd offered to be auctioned off for
dinner on Valentine's Day.

When number twenty took the stage, Maggie's mouth
dropped open in astonishment. His name was Matt Lindstrom. As shock registered through her that this was the man
she'd accidently walked into, she listened intently to the MC
with her eyes glued to the screen and the man in front of it.
He was CEO of Lindstrom Financial, one of the largest
Minnesota financial companies in the state. Suddenly he was
speaking and their eyes locked through the crowd. At least
she thought they had, but how could one tell in a crowded
room? Heck it could be someone behind her he was boldly
staring at. One thing she knew for sure though, was her
mother was staring back at her and hadn't missed the
shocked look on her face.

Damn! She didn't stand a chance, because at that
moment, she knew Matt was the bachelor her mother was
going to bid on. And seeing the look of obvious longing on
Maggie's face would ensure her mother would win.

Maggie felt a wave of uneasiness wash over her. She

wanted nothing more than to exit the room and go home. And totally bow out of the whole date thing. But was that what she really wanted? Part of her truly wanted to have that date with Matt. If only to see if the attraction she felt towards him was mutual.

She could hardly sit still. Her hands were clasped tightly in her lap. Maggie watched as the men walked on stage one at a time and the bidding commenced. Her mother had not bid on any of them. It was now the last bachelor, Matt, who stood on the stage. The other bachelors had been able to raise between five to ten thousand dollars each. Matt's auction opened with a bid from her mother for ten thousand dollars. The room oohed and became silent waiting to hear if there were any other bids. None came.

"Once, twice and the winning bid goes to Margit Johnson," the auctioneer called out.

Her mother won the date.

Maggie covered her face with her hands. She wasn't sure if she should be mad as hell or forever thankful. But either way, she was out of there. Luckily, the crowd was beginning to disperse. Swiftly, she got up and made her way to the coat check ahead of the rush. She dropped a five dollar bill in the tip jar and walked toward the front doors. She had to leave.

The valet took the ticket from her and ran off to get her car.

Since it was snowing again and still windy, she buttoned all the buttons on her coat this time to stop the shivering. Although she wasn't certain it was from the cold.

The valet pulled up with her car, she handed him a ten dollar bill, got in and left the Lafayette in her rear view mirror. Moments later, her phone rang and she pressed a button to answer the hands free phone system. "Hello, Mother."

"Maggie, where are you?"

"I had to go. I'm on my way home."

"Are you okay, Maggie?"

"Yes, I'll be fine. It was just a bit too surreal for me."

"You will go on the date with Matt, won't you?"

"Yes, Mom. I said I would, so I will. I need to go now. I'll call you tomorrow."

CHAPTER 4

*M*att was obligated to meet the woman who'd won the bid for a Valentine's date with him. While he descended the stage steps, he saw the beautiful blonde woman who'd accidentally pressed her sensuous body against his only hours earlier, make a quick exit out of the building. Damn, but he was intrigued by her. She was stunningly gorgeous and he wanted to formally be introduced to her, so he could ask her out on a date.

Matt shook Margit's hand. "So happy to meet you, Margit Johnson. And thank you for your very generous donation to the Children's Hospital Heart Center. Your donation along with the others will make a huge impact on their research efforts."

"It's definitely a worthy cause that I heartily support." Margit smiled.

"I look forward to dinner at Lord Fletchers." Matt wasn't really looking forward to it, but he flashed her one of his charismatic smiles.

"Yes, it should be an interesting evening." Margit turned

away and walked towards her friend, Nancy, who was waiting for her by the door.

Matt nodded and walked over to his waiting Dad.

"Matt." Carl put his arm around his shoulders. "At least it will be an easy dinner."

"That's for sure. Won't get you any grandchildren though." Matt smiled and soon, both he and his dad were immersed in laughter.

"You do need to work on that, though," Carl chided.

"Actually, ran into someone tonight who did interest me, but unfortunately she ran off before I could get her phone number."

"Maybe they have her on video." Carl couldn't stop a huge hopeful smile from spreading across his face.

"What?" Matt asked.

"They videotaped the program, remember?" Carl questioned.

"For real?"

"Yes. You really should read forms before you sign them." Carl reprimanded his son.

"I'll check to see if I can get a copy of it sent to me. Maybe someone will know her name." Matt was hopeful that this crazy auction could work to his benefit, yet.

Later that night, as he lay in his bed, his head filled with visions of the woman he'd run into, her sexy body wrapped in his arms while kissing full luscious lips. And he intended to use everything in his power to find her.

Maggie tossed and turned the whole night long. At least it seemed like it was hours and hours. She couldn't stop thinking about the upcoming date with Matt. The mere touch of her hand on his chest, accidentally of course, had spawned a yearning inside her body she hadn't felt for a long time. Why did it have to be for a total stranger? Chemistry is chemistry and something you don't really have any control over. Odds were that he didn't feel the same. She didn't think she could get that lucky. There was only one way to find out, though, just go on the date, and play it cool. Act nonchalant and see how he reacted.

He seemed like a really nice person from what she had observed when he spoke to the audience at the auction. There had to be something wrong with him, though, that he was still an eligible bachelor at thirty-five. He was extremely good looking, owned his own company, obviously had money, so why would he still be single? Probably, one of those guys who didn't want to have just one girlfriend and definitely didn't want to get married. Oh hell! Why was she even thinking about marriage? She didn't know if she wanted to go that route again, so what did it matter if he didn't?

One thing she did know for sure, she wanted to make a good impression, either way. Although, she didn't have anything to wear for a Valentine's Day date. *A red dress.* That's what she needed. A sexy, provocative but classy red dress. Along with matching shoes, purse and jewelry, too! Annie needed to go shopping with her tomorrow. She would call her in the morning to set up a time.

Since she had everything figured out now, she just might be able to fall asleep.

~

Nine o'clock sharp, Maggie's phone rang. She'd just finished showering and walked over to her night stand to pick up her phone. It was her mother. "Hello, Mother."

"Maggie, did you sleep well?"

"Not really."

"I always tell you that you worry about things too much. Everything will be fine."

"Sure you can say that because you aren't the one going on a date with a strange man."

"Well, he's not exactly a stranger. You did kind of meet him last night. You did listen to his bio?"

"Yes, Mother. He sounds like a perfectly nice guy."

"Glad to hear you say that. I'm sure he will be good company for the dinner. And dance."

"You never mentioned a dance."

"It's a formal dinner with a band, so I'm assuming there will be a dance floor. Is that a problem? I know you used to like to go dancing."

"I took Ballroom Dance classes. Doesn't mean he did, though."

"Regardless, it should be a night to remember. Do you have a red dress?"

"No. I've already called Annie and we're going shopping this afternoon."

"Great! Send me the bill. After all it's my fault you need a red dress, so I'm happy to cover it."

"Gotta go now, Mom. Talk to you, later."

Maggie finished dressing and headed out to run some errands and grab a little breakfast at Starbucks.

She arrived at the Mall of America just before one and made her way to Tinucci's restaurant. Annie was seated at a patio table waiting. Maggie took a seat across from her.

"So, I want to hear all about last night. I'm assuming your mother won the bid on one of the bachelors since we're shopping for a red dress."

"Of course, she did. Was there ever any doubt?"

Annie clapped her hands. "None whatsoever. So give. Who is he?"

"Matt Lindstrom, CEO of Lindstrom Financial."

"Really. That is impressive. Did you google him?"

"No, why. They read his bio at the event. He actually sounds like a nice guy."

Annie pulled out her phone and googled his name. "They all sound nice at first."

"Seriously, you're going to look him up?"

"Of course, I am."

"What do you hope to find? It's not going to say he's a jerk and no one should go out on a date with him."

"No, but wouldn't it be nice if it did?" Annie intently read the info about Matt that came up on her phone. "It says he went to Wayzata High School, graduated four years ahead of us. That's why we don't recognize the name."

"Where did he go to college?"

"It says University of St. Thomas with a Masters in Finance."

"That makes sense if he has a financial company."

"Oh my, he is definitely hot. Totally GQ material. If you don't want to go, I will gladly take your place."

"No, thanks. I'm going."

"Wow. That's a total change of attitude. Did something happen you're not telling me about?"

"Yes. I accidentally walked right into him. And, Annie, I felt sparks. I didn't know he was one of the bachelors at the time. Imagine my shock when he walked on stage as number twenty."

"Let me get this straight. You told your mother to bid on him?"

"No, but she saw my face when he walked on stage. Not sure, but I might've shown my interest at that point. He's a definite ten."

"That explains everything. There was no way anyone was going to outbid your mother on number twenty."

"Exactly."

"So we need to find you a red dress and accessories?" Annie picked up her glass of White Zinfandel the waitress had just brought to the table.

Maggie raised hers and they lifted them in a toast. "To Matt, may he be a truly nice guy."

After taking a sip, Annie asked, "By the way does he know the date is with you and not your mother, since she was the one who did the bidding?"

"Dang! Didn't even think of that. Knowing my mother, she didn't tell him, so it will be a total surprise. I'll have to ask her."

"This date could prove quite interesting. Wish I could watch it unfold. Maybe they will film it?"

"I'm pretty sure they're not."

"I did read in the paper that they filmed the auction, but it will be a few days maybe a week before it will be available for viewing on their website."

CHAPTER 5

*M*att had waited as patiently as possible for the Valentine's auction committee to post the video for the event on their website. Finally, a week later, he'd received an email from his dad that it was up. Once on the website he saw the video appear on the homepage. Wow, it was thirty minutes long, which hopefully meant they had included footage from the audience. He tapped on the arrow and the video started. Twenty minutes into it, he finally saw her. He pressed pause. Yes, it was her. That still didn't tell him who she was, though. It was Saturday and he was on his way out anyway, so he decided to stop at his Dad's house.

It still brought back sad memories when he drove up to his family's home. His mother had lost her battle with cancer five years ago, so now his dad lived in the stately mansion alone. Once inside, he brought up the website on his dad's computer and they sat down to watch it.

"By the way, you look great on this film, Matt."

"Thanks, Dad." He pressed pause as he came to her beautiful face. It actually appeared that she was a bit shocked to see him on stage. Then it panned to the bidders, Margit, in particular. "Do you recognize her?" he asked pointing to the woman who'd been haunting his dreams for the past week.

"No. But I do remember the woman bidding from years ago. I didn't recognize her that night, but now I do. She looks different than when we were in high school. At Wayzata." Carl stared at the screen.

"Really?" Matt asked.

"Yes, she actually lives on Grey's Bay. I remember her husband died in a car accident about ten years ago. He was in Real Estate and did quite well. I'm sure he had her well taken care of in case anything happened to him. If I recall correctly from the obituary, he had a daughter who would be a bit younger than you."

Matt googled Margit Johnson on his phone. Sure enough she had a daughter who would be about thirty. The young woman could possibly be her, but it was hard to say since it was most likely a high school picture that had popped up. He showed the picture to his dad.

"She sure is pretty. Do you think that is the girl you ran into?"

"Possibly. The Valentine's dinner date could prove interesting. I can ask Margit if her daughter was at the auction. I just might find myself looking forward to this dinner. And this Valentine's Day may just be one to remember."

"Good. That's the attitude I like to see in you. Keep thinking grand-babies."

"Sure, Dad. I'll put that at the top of my list of things to do." They both laughed, but he knew his dad was serious.

Matt left to finish his errands and meet up with the guys for dinner. Sunday was the Vikings football game with friends in his company's suite at the new Vikings Stadium. Then, only a few days until his big date.

❧

The week passed by quickly at her office. Sandvik Mortgage was a company her mother started after her dad passed away ten years ago. Sandvik was her mother's maiden name so it seemed appropriate to use for the name of their new company. Margit had processed mortgages for over twenty years for Tower Mortgage. When the owner, Don Madsen, wanted to retire, he offered to sell the company to her mother. That's how it became a family business that Maggie and Margit owned and operated in Wayzata. Since Valentine's Day was on a Saturday this year, she was certain that Bachman's Flower truck would show up on Friday. So she made sure to take the day off. Instead, she and Annie were having a girl's spa day at Opus Spa. Facials, massages, manicure, pedicure, the whole works. Then, dinner at Maynard's.

Friday had turned out to be a bright sunny day with temps in the mid-forties. Extremely unusual for February. They couldn't resist walking out to the shore of Lake Minnetonka before going inside Maynard's for dinner. The lake was covered with over twenty inches of snow and the top layer resembled ice crystals sparkling like diamonds in the vibrant sun.

She loved the lake. She'd grown up on this lake and it was a part of her forever. Some of her friends moved away, like Liv, choosing oceans on either coast or the mountains of Denver, but not her. Minnesota was her home and this lake was where she belonged and wanted to stay. This had always been in the back of her mind when she met a new man, whether he would stay in Minnesota or want to move away to someplace warmer.

Maggie needed a man who loved Minnesota as much as she did. She knew she was looking too far ahead, where Matt was concerned, but he was a born and bred Minnesotan who had a company headquartered in Minnesota. He'd been so devastatingly handsome and she'd felt chemistry with him.

The man seemed perfect. Now, she only needed to see if he felt the same.

So much hope and lifelong dreams rested on a simple dinner date at Lord Fletcher's on Valentine's Day.

Matt managed to pull a profile on Maggie Johnson complete with a picture, which he'd printed out. He'd even gone so far as to set the picture on his desk. Every day he grew more excited to meet her. If he proved completely and flawlessly gallant on his date with her mother, he was sure she would introduce him to her daughter, Maggie.

Finally, it was Saturday. Matt had dressed in his GQ tux for the special occasion. He wanted to make a good impression on Margit. The bachelors needed to arrive early at Lord Fletcher's for pictures, so he would be on his way shortly.

CHAPTER 6

 aggie took her time with her make-up and hair. She hadn't been this nervous about a date in years. She'd had her long blonde tresses gently curled at the salon this afternoon and was just about ready to put on the crimson red brocade dress with a deep V neck. It had long sleeves and the hem was slightly above her knees. Then, she slipped on her black three-inch pumps. After hooking her large ruby pendant necklace, a gift for her eighteenth birthday from her father, she took one last glance in the mirror. Her reflection was a snapshot that could only be captioned as 'beautiful classy young woman.' At least, this would be what she was aiming for.

On the short drive to Fletcher's, she couldn't help hoping Matt would be okay with having her for his date instead of her mother. When she pulled up, she saw there was a line of cars. She got in line and watched as each woman was greeted by a host from the auction and ushered inside. Her mother had made the changes from her name to Maggie's, so hopefully there wouldn't be any problem.

It was her turn, so she pulled forward. The valet opened

her door and handed her a ticket. Tonight, she left her coat in the car and walked toward the entrance door.

Once inside, she was greeted by the MC from the auction. "Maggie Johnson, I presume?" he asked.

"Yes." Maggie was relieved to hear her name instead of her mother's.

"This way." He motioned towards an open door filled with the bachelors and women who were their dates.

"Your date is Matt Lindstrom. If you will follow me, I'll introduce you."

Maggie felt her stomach tighten, but she wouldn't let her nerves get the best of her. She took a deep breath and followed him to where she saw Matt standing.

"Matt, I'd like to introduce you to Maggie Johnson. She is taking the place of her mother, Margit, who placed the winning bid for your dinner date."

Matt's face lit up. "Maggie, I'm extremely pleased to meet you." He extended his hand to shake hers.

She felt the chemistry ignite between them. Did he feel it, too? She couldn't help smiling at him. "Pleased to meet you, Matt. Hope you don't mind me as your substitute dinner date?"

"Not at all. I'm pleasantly surprised. Would you care for a drink?" He grinned and pointed towards the bar.

"Yes, that would be nice. Perhaps a glass of wine. Blush."

At the bar, Matt ordered her a Blush wine and a Boudreaux for himself. They walked over to a high top table and set their glasses down after taking a sip.

"I wanted to talk to you that night after the auction, but you disappeared rather quickly." Matt stared into her eyes.

"After our accidental meeting and my mother bidding on the date with you, I felt a bit overwhelmed." Maggie decided being up front was the best course of action at this point. "Why did you want to talk to me?"

"I wanted to introduce myself and hopefully talk you into going out to dinner with me sometime."

"Why?"

"I felt an immediate connection with you that night. The attraction was strong and I guess I wanted to see if you felt it, too." Matt admitted and intently watched her face for a response.

Just then, the MC holding the mic instructed everyone to proceed into the ballroom to be seated for dinner. Each table had the bachelor's number, so they proceeded to number twenty.

Matt pulled out her chair like a perfect gentleman and then took his seat across from her.

She knew she hadn't answered his question, but wanted the opportunity to get to know him better before she answered. He would get his answer before the night was over, though.

"I heard in your bio that you attended Wayzata High School," Maggie stated.

"I did. And you?"

"Wayzata, also. You are a few years older I suspect, which is why we didn't know each other then."

"I'm thirty-five. And you?" Matt volunteered.

"Thirty-one." Maggie hoped he wasn't looking for someone younger.

"So we both grew up here in Wayzata and never met. That's unfortunate. I think we may have a lot in common," Matt concluded.

"I love it here in Wayzata. I wouldn't dream of living anywhere else."

"My company is here and this is my home. I'm planning on staying in Minnesota. Sometimes winters get rough, but that's what vacations are for. It's nice to get away from the cold, but I'm always glad to get back home." Matt watched her intently, seeming to take in everything about her.

Maggie smiled. Yes, she liked what she was hearing. "I have a company here, too. I love getting away to Mexico for a couple of weeks in January, but Minnesota is home."

hrough their full five course dinner, they talked about their lives and dreams. Dessert was a lavish chocolate heart shaped cake for two with a fresh coating of chocolate glaze frosting, garnished with two large strawberries.

A local band, Tonka Buccaneers, played jazzy blues style music while they ate. The dance floor was opened for dancing after dessert was served.

"Would you like to dance?" Matt asked.

"Sure," Maggie said and stood up to follow him onto the dance floor.

He swept her into his arms and proceeded to direct her in a ballroom swing style dance. She followed along gracefully matching his steps, step for step. They flowed across the dance floor as one.

After a couple of songs they made their way back to their table.

"That was fun. You are quite well versed in the Ballroom Dance steps," Matt complimented her.

"Yes, I was a dancer since I was three, but it wasn't too useful after high school. A few of my college friends decided Ballroom Dancing would be fun, so we took classes. With our dance backgrounds, we were able to pick it up easily. How about you? You are quite good." Maggie couldn't help smiling. She was so happy she was on a Valentine's Day date with him.

"My mother is to blame. Bless her heart. We lost her a few years back to cancer, but it is because of her I took the classes. She signed up me and my dad. Mom said it was something we needed to learn and something we could use our whole lives. So we did. I found I really enjoyed it and for me too, it came naturally."

People had left the room couple by couple for the last hour. They were the last ones left.

"I think they are waiting for us to leave," Matt said nodding towards the empty room.

"Yes, it appears so."

Matt pulled out his business card and handed it to Maggie. "Here's my number and I'd love to get yours."

Maggie pulled out her business card and handed it to Matt.

"I will call you. I would love for us to get to know each other better. I think we have a lot in common," Matt promised.

"That would be great," Maggie responded and smiled.

They went outside and waited for the valet to pull up their cars.

"You never did answer my question from earlier." Matt waited intently to hear her answer.

"I know. I was waiting. The answer is yes, I felt it, too."

With that answer, Matt pulled Maggie into his arms for a gentle seeking kiss that ignited between them, a spark of passion, a love just beginning to bloom. He released her. "Would tomorrow be too soon?" he asked.

Maggie felt her cheeks flush. "Tomorrow would be great." Once again, her heart was filled with hopes for a bright future. This was definitely going to be a Valentine's Day she would always remember. Her purse vibrated from her phone. She pulled it out to look and see who was texting her, just as Matt's phone vibrated in his pocket.

Maggie saw the words *'Marriage Possibilities?'* on the screen from her mother. She laughed.

Matt read the words *'Grand-babies?'* on his screen from his dad. He laughed.

They both put their phones away.

Matt gazed at Maggie.

"Just my mother," she explained and looked over at Matt.

"Just my dad." He nodded as he grinned.

Matt couldn't resist pulling her into his arms once more for a good-night kiss as the valet pulled up with her car. Reluctantly, he released her and helped her walk around to the driver's side of the car. After she was seated, he closed the door for her. She put the window down and smiled up at Matt who was still standing beside her car.

"Hope your Valentine's Day Bachelor Date was everything you'd hoped for."

"Best Valentine's Day date, *ever*." Maggie slowly put the window up and headed home. She couldn't wait for his call tomorrow. The anticipation alone, might keep her awake all night! Hopefully, she would never have to dread Valentine's Day, *ever*, again. She had a really good feeling about Matt and she would definitely have to thank her Mom tomorrow.

Matt's face was beaming. He walked over to his car that the valet had just parked next to him as he watched her drive away.

Little did Matt, Maggie, Carl or Margit know that this Valentine's Day would be a life changing event for all of them. Marriage and a baby would be in the near future binding them all together for a lifetime.

RECIPE

FLOURLESS CHOCOLATE HEART CAKE

Ingredients

- 1 pound dark chocolate, chopped
- 16 tablespoons unsalted butter
- 8 large eggs
- Powdered sugar, optional
- Raspberries, optional
- *(Makes 9-inch Cake)*

To Prepare:

1. Preheat oven to 325 degrees. Grease 9-inch heart shaped, cake or Spring-form pan, set aside.
2. In a large microwave safe bowl, add chocolate and butter. Heat on high for 1 minute, remove and stir. Repeat one time, or until chocolate is smooth and creamy, set aside.
3. In stand mixer or large bowl, beat eggs until frothy and slightly thickened. Add chocolate mixture and mix on low for 1 minute. Pour into prepared pan

and place inside a roasting pan. Place pan in oven and fill with hot water around perimeter until it reaches halfway up sides of pan.

4. Bake for 20-25 minutes, just until set. Remove and let cool for 30 minutes. Using a knife, loosen edges and invert onto plate. Sprinkle with powdered sugar and serve with berries, if desired or use a chocolate glaze frosting. Enjoy!

ABOUT THE AUTHOR

ROSE MARIE MEUWISSEN

Rose Marie Meuwissen, a first-generation Norwegian American born and raised in Minnesota, always tries to incorporate her Norwegian heritage into her writing. After receiving a BA in Marketing from Concordia University, a Masters in Creative Writing from Hamline University soon followed. Minnesota is still where she calls home.

She has traveled around the world, including Scandinavia, but still has many places to see, enjoys attending Scandinavian events, writing conferences and is usually busy writing Minnesota Lakes Contemporary Romances, Viking Time Travel Romances or Norwegian Traditions Children's Books.

Visit her at www.rosemariemeuwissen.com or www.realnorwegianseatlutefisk.com.

NOVELS:

- *Taking Chances*—a contemporary romance novel set in Minnesota and Arizona.
- *Married by Saturday*—a contemporary romance novel set in Minnesota and Montana.
- *Looking for Mr. Right*—a contemporary internet dating romance novel set on Prior Lake in Minnesota—*Coming soon!*

NOVELLAS:

- *Annika—A Christmas Romance*—a contemporary romance set in Minnesota with a Nordic theme during the Christmas Holidays.
- *Skol! Viking Blonde Ale*—a contemporary romance set in Minnesota at an Autumn festival complete with a fortune teller, ale and Vikings!
- *Choosing to Live*—a Norwegian woman's journey during WWII to survive the Nazi Occupation of Norway—*Coming soon!*

MINNESOTA LAKES ROMANCE NOVELETTES:

- *A Kiss Under the Northern Lights*—a Summer romance set in Ely, Minnesota on Big Lake.
- *Dancing in the Moonlight*—a Summer romance set in Malmo, Minnesota on Mille Lacs Lake.
- *Hot Summer Nights*—a Summer romance set in Prior Lake, Minnesota on Prior Lake.
- *Railroad Ties*—an Autumn romance set in Two Harbors, Minnesota on Lake Superior.
- *Blizzard of Love*—a Winter romance set in Lutsen, Minnesota on Lake Superior.
- *Nor-Way to Love*—a Spring romance set in Minneapolis, Minnesota on Lake Harriet.
- *Old Yule Log Fires*—a Christmas romance set in Excelsior, Minnesota on Lake Minnetonka.
- *A Date for Valentine's Day*—a Valentine romance set in Minnetonka Beach, Minnesota at the Lafayette Country Club on Lake Minnetonka.
- *Dance of Love*—a Fall Festival romance set at the Renaissance Fair in Shakopee, Minnesota.

CHILDREN'S BOOKS—

REAL NORWEGIAN'S SERIES:

- *Real Norwegians Eat Lutefisk*—a Children's book about the tradition of Lutefisk presented in both English and Norwegian.
- *Real Norwegians Eat Rømmegrøt*—the second Children's book in the series about the tradition of Rømmegrøt presented in both English and Norwegian.
- *Real Norwegians Eat Lefse*—the third Children's book in the series about the tradition of Lefse presented in both English and Norwegian.
- *Real Norwegians Eat Krumkake*—the fourth Children's book in the series about the tradition of Krumkake presented in both English and Norwegian—*Coming next!*

MICRO-MINI NOVELETTE—COMING SOON!

- *Christmas Notes*—a collection of Christmas prose poems to warm the heart during the Christmas season.

CONTINUE READING FOR A
PREVIEW OF:

ANNIKA—A CHRISTMAS ROMANCE
Betting on Paris Series
By
Rose Marie Meuwissen

ANNIKA—A CHRISTMAS ROMANCE

BETTING ON PARIS SERIES

ISBN 978-0-9903788-4-6
Published in the United States of America
Nordic Publishing LLC
Cover Design by Angie Speed

INTRODUCTION

Spend the holidays with Josie, Ryley, Emma, Alana, and Annika. Get ready for five weeks of romance with a new Christmas series brought to you by five exciting contemporary authors...

Betting on Paris!

Five exciting stories linked by a unifying theme. You'll want to read each one!

BETTING ON PARIS SERIES

Sometimes the best bet is the one you lose...

Five best friends. Five promises.

Each year in mid-August, the former college roommates meet up on a girls-only trip somewhere in the world. This year, it's Paris, the city of museums, art and romance. On the last night of their vacation, the girls engage in a serious talk about the sorry state of their love lives and collectively decide they are swearing off men. Instead, each woman is intent on pursuing her life's goal. Falling in love is the *last* thing on her mind!

This is **Annika's** story...

Owning Nordic Travel and Tours was a dream come true and Annika certainly didn't have time for romance. So why had she met the man of her dreams, now?

Tristan's Minnesota Events and Adventures Company for singles allowed him the ability to meet available women on a regular basis, so why would he be interested in her?

Annika had never mixed business with pleasure before and since Tristan would be booking tours through her company, there would be no romance. Now, she only had to convince her heart.

Find all the Betting on Paris novellas at Amazon!

Josie by Beth Gildersleeve
Ryley by Donna Lovitz
Emma by Angie Wilder
Alana by Denise Devine
Annika by Rose Marie Meuwissen

ANNIKA — CHAPTER ONE

$\mathcal{A}$fter driving around the parking ramp for what seemed like an eternity, Annika pulled her SUV into an empty spot and quickly unloaded two medium-sized plastic tubs onto her wheeled cart, then hurried toward the glassed-in elevator. Plopping her purse down on top of the tubs, she pressed the button for the main level while her eyes focused on her phone to check the time. *Only thirty minutes until the doors open for the Minneapolis Travel Expo at the convention center.*

She took a couple of calming breaths, trying to erase visions of the backed up freeway she'd just spent way too much time on during the morning rush hour traffic. Thank God, she lived and worked in the suburbs! Absolutely no way, would she put herself through that rat race every day to get to work. The door opened and she backed out of the elevator pulling the cart with her, but stopped abruptly when she felt a firm pressure on her back. The top bin went crashing to the floor sending her travel brochures into a very messy pile beside her cart. She turned around quickly to see what had stopped her dead in her tracks.

Piercing blue eyes and sandy blond hair focused on her.

Her face flushed in embarrassment. "I'm so sorry. I'm in a hurry and wasn't watching what or who was behind me as I backed out of the elevator."

He grinned at her, sliding his phone into his pocket and bent down to retrieve a handful of brochures. "I can't let you take all the blame. I was on my phone and not paying attention to my surroundings, either. Let me help you." He picked up more of the fallen brochures and placed them into the plastic container.

Annika picked up the remaining brochures setting them in the bin, carefully placing the cover over the top, pressing down until she heard the click signifying it was on tightly. "Thank you. I do have to run though." She turned and quickly walked into the main ballroom with her cart in tow after flashing the security guard her exhibitor nametag.

Thankfully, the booth had already been set up last night by her assistant, Holly, who would be arriving around noon after her prenatal doctor's appointment. Annika hadn't a clue what she would do without Holly for three months, maybe more, while she was out on maternity leave. The baby was due in October which was coming up way too soon.

They'd been late getting the newly designed brochures to the printer, only being able to pick them up yesterday afternoon which was why she'd been hauling them into the Expo this morning. She neatly arranged them on the table, and then sat down on the comfortably padded chair to reign in her emotions after her collision in the hallway. Typically, she didn't do things like that, but today she was off her normal routine after dealing with the traffic and rushing to get into the Expo before the event started and the doors opened.

Well, she'd made it with a few minutes to spare. She picked up a bottle of water, left at the table for them by the Expo, and downed almost half of it, wanting to stay hydrated since she was about to do a lot of talking to potential customers and clients.

The guy she'd bumped into was definitely good looking, but she'd sworn off men for a year to concentrate on her business. Recently, on a trip to Paris with her best friends, Alana, Josie, Ryley and Emma, they'd all made a pact to focus on their jobs and to not let *any* men interfere with their career plans for a year. *Betting on Paris—No Men for a Year* was their pact slogan. Besides, her dream of owning her own travel tour company, Nordic Travel and Tours, had come true after the first of the year, when her boss, Dan Nystad, retired and sold it to her. Dan felt she was the best person to run the company and take it to the next step into the tech future of the twenty first century. He'd been a friend and mentor, teaching her everything about travel and tours for the past ten years of her career. She needed no distractions this year, especially, to make all the transitions needed to take her company into the new tech age, for which, it was sorely lacking.

At nine o'clock on the dot, the Expo's doors opened and people rushed in, eager to find all the freebies like pens, hats and bags, but hopefully there would be many who wanted to book tours and were serious about traveling in Minnesota and other places in the world, like Scandinavia, which was her specialty. Her booth would be giving away pens and brochures imprinted with photos of exciting cities and places to visit.

Soon, the aisles were full of people and many stopped at her booth to gaze at the breathtaking photos of the fjords of Norway on the promotional banners. Nothing could match their beauty. She handed out brochures and answered questions, trying to remember to take sips of water in between potential clients.

Holly arrived at noon carrying what appeared to be her lunch along with a large purse filled with necessities for the long day. "I made it." Holly sat down on the chair.

"I hope you didn't have to walk very far."

"No, I got a spot in the parking ramp, but at seven months pregnant any walking takes extra effort."

"Go ahead and eat your lunch and when you're done, I'll go get something from the food vendors."

Annika continued talking with the people walking through the Expo until Holly finished eating.

Holly stood up and walked to the counter. "I'm done so go ahead and get some lunch. Bet you didn't have any breakfast and are starving." She shooed Annika out of the booth.

Tristan watched the woman walk away. She definitely had poise and class, and appeared to be very professional. *Extremely attractive, too.* He was intrigued, but this was a work day and he was on a mission today. His Minnesota Events and Adventures Company, for singles seeking new friends and adventure in the Midwest and abroad, needed a tour company. Leisurely, he made his way toward the coffee kiosk, since the doors wouldn't open for another twenty minutes. He felt confident in finding the perfect tour company for his company's travel needs today, if his gut feeling was accurate and it usually was.

Finally, when the doors opened for the Expo, Tristan walked up to the counter and greeted Holly. "Hi, I think this might be exactly what I'm looking for." He picked up a brochure which oddly looked familiar.

"Well, that would make my job easier." Holly laughed.

"What can Nordic Travel and Tours do for you and your company?"

"My company is Minnesota Events and Adventures for singles. We set up events and travel destinations for our members. I'm looking for a company that can set up the tours and travel parts for us to sell as a group package to our clients. Basically, my company gets the people and your company would set everything up."

"This could be a perfect match because what we do is all the planning for trips such as the air, hotels, transportation and tours."

Tristan picked up a business card from the counter. "Are you Annika?"

"No, I'm Holly. Annika Karlstad is the owner and manager of the company and I'm her assistant." She pulled out her IPad with Annika's calendar. "I think you'd probably like to talk to her in person, so she can go over everything in detail. I have her calendar up on my IPad, so I'd be happy to set up an appointment next week for you."

Tristan pulled out his phone from his pocket and brought up his calendar. "Would Tuesday work?"

"She has a ten o'clock slot open."

"That should work." He pulled out his business card and handed it to Holly. "My name is Tristan Torgersen and I look forward to meeting Ms. Karlstad."

Holly smiled as she watched Tristan move on down the aisle past the rows of vendors.

Annika regretted not bringing a lunch when she saw the prices and the menu. Not that she had much choice at this point, so she ordered a salad and ice tea. While she waited for her food she checked her phone for any messages.

"So we meet again."

She turned to see who spoke. It was the man she'd literally run into earlier. "Hello. Again."

"How is the rest of your day going?"

"Much better. How about you?" Annika asked.

"Already made it half way through the auditorium. I think I've already found what I was looking for though."

"Oh, so will you still walk through the other half?"

"I'm here, so might as well take a look in case some other company strikes my fancy." Tristan chuckled.

"Well, best of luck…I guess I never got your name."

"Tristan."

"Well then Tristan, I'm Annika. Hope you find what you're looking for at the Travel Expo."

"I think I already may have found exactly what I'm looking for, Annika." Tristan smiled.

Annika heard her number called. "That's me. It's been nice running into you again." She gave him her best smile, then walked up to the counter to pick up her food. Discreetly, she positioned herself, so she could see if he'd left.

Tristan caught her eyes drifting his direction and tipped his head slightly in a nod, turned and walked back into the auditorium.

Why she felt so flustered around this guy, she had no idea. Her heart was racing and she knew she wanted to see him again. She knew nothing about him, so it was utterly ridiculous to be feeling this way. Besides, she wasn't looking for someone to date. At least not this year anyway, because she needed to stay focused on her company. She was personally responsible for making it a success. She didn't need any distractions.

After she'd finished eating her lunch, she made her way down a couple of aisles to check out the competition before going back to her booth. She felt confident about her company and what they had to offer clients. They offered bus tours to events and destinations in Minnesota and even some to the neighboring states of Wisconsin, Iowa, South Dakota and North Dakota. The tours to Scandinavia had always been top rated by their customers because they were unique in offering many off the beaten path options which were sought after by those with Scandinavian ancestry.

"Did I miss anything?" Annika asked taking a seat next to Holly.

"I put a couple of appointments on your calendar for next week that I think might be great new clients and handed out quite a few of the brochures."

"Tell me about the appointments."

"One is for a company looking to book some flight packages for their sales people who made their goals. And one is for the local company, Minnesota Events and Adventures. The company is for singles and they book group travel in and out of Minnesota for their events."

"Good job, Holly. Those sound like they have great potential for us."

A group of young people walked up to the table to ask about the trips to Iceland. Annika eagerly became engaged in conversation revolving around her passion for travel to the Scandinavian countries.

www.ingramcontent.com/pod-product-compliance
Lightning Source LLC
Chambersburg PA
CBHW022052170626
46808CB00003B/1444